Sprite's Secret

D1054016

Pixie Tricks

Read All the Magical Adventures!

Pixie Tricks

Sprite's Secret

Written by
Tracey West

Illustrated by
Xavier Bonet

BRANCHES™
SCHOLASTIC INC.

This one's for the fairies. — TW

For my children, Daniel and Marti.
You're pure magic. — XB

Text copyright © 2000, 2020 by Tracey West
Illustrations copyright © 2020 by Xavier Bonet

All rights reserved. Published by Scholastic Inc., *Publishers since 1920.* SCHOLASTIC, BRANCHES, and associated logos are trademarks and/or registered trademarks of Scholastic Inc.

Library of Congress Cataloging-in-Publication Data
Names: West, Tracey, 1965- author. | Bonet, Xavier, illustrator. | West, Tracey, 1965- Pixie tricks ; 1. Title: Sprite's secret / written by Tracey West ; illustrated by Xavier Bonet.
Description: [New edition, with new illustrations] | New York : Branches/Scholastic Inc., 2020. | Series: Pixie tricks; 1 | Originally published: New York : Scholastic, ©2000. | Summary: Fourteen fairies have escaped into our world, all different, and all capable of causing great harm—and it is up to an eight-year-old girl named Violet and a Pixie Tricker, a fairy called Sprite-of-the-Green-Petals-from-the-Whispering-Woods, to trick them and send them back to their own world.

Identifiers: LCCN 2019028151 (print) | LCCN 2019028152 (ebook) |
ISBN 9781338627787 (paperback) | ISBN 9781338627794 (library binding) | ISBN 9781338627800 (ebk) Subjects: LCSH: Fairies—Juvenile fiction. | Games—Juvenile fiction. | CYAC: Fairies—Fiction. | Games—Fiction. Classification: LCC PZ7.W51937 Sq 2020 (print) | DDC 813.54 [Fic]—dc23
LC record available at https://lccn.loc.gov/2019028151

10 9 8 7 6 5 4 3 2 1   20 21 22 23 24

Printed in China   62
This edition first printing, December 2020
Book design by Sarah Dvojack

Table of Contents

Whenever pixies do escape
Through the old oak tree,
Here is what you have to do
Or trouble there will be.
First find a Pixie Tricker,
The youngest in the land.
Send him to the human world,
The Book of Tricks in hand.
Once he's there, he'll find a girl
Who's only eight years old.
But she's a smart and clever girl
Who's also very bold.
He must ask her for her help,
And if she does agree,
They'll trick the pixies one by one
Till no more do they see.
Only they can do the job.
It's much more than a game.
For if they fail to trick them all,
The world won't be the same!

1

A Marble and a Toad

"Give me back my marble!"

Violet Briggs was yelling at a toad. The toad hopped away from her. It held a large marble in its mouth.

It was Violet's favorite marble. The best one in her collection. She had been in her backyard playing with the marbles. Then the toad came. It picked up the marble and hopped away.

"Come back here!" Violet yelled.

Violet chased the toad. It hopped across the green grass. Violet reached for it. She almost had it . . .

Hop! It landed on a rock.

Violet reached out again.

Hop! It landed on a small patch of yellow buttercups.

Violet tried to grab it . . .

Hop! The toad landed on the roots of an old oak tree.

Violet stopped running. She got down on her knees. The damp grass soaked through her pants.

The toad sat still on the roots of the tree.

Slowly, Violet crawled to the toad.

"I don't want to hurt you," she whispered. "I just want my marble back!"

Violet held out her hand. She was so close! She could almost touch the toad's brown, bumpy skin.

Hop! The toad hopped right into a hole in the tree trunk and disappeared.

"No!" Violet cried. She looked inside the hole.

A face looked back at her.

But it wasn't a frog face. In fact, it wasn't the face of an animal at all! It was the face of a tiny person.

2
A Fairy?

Violet jumped back. The tiny person flew out of the hole. He floated in the air in front of Violet's face.

"Hello there," he said.

Violet tried to speak. But she couldn't. Not yet. She stared at the little creature.

He was about as tall as a pencil. He had green eyes and pointy ears. His skin was pale green. And his hair was a very light yellow.

Violet thought his clothes were made from leaves. But the most amazing thing about him was his wings. They shimmered in the air. They looked like they were made of rainbows.

"I said, HELLO!" said the creature.

Violet closed her eyes. She *must* be seeing things.

Violet counted to three.

She opened her eyes.

The creature was still there.

"Are you all right?" he asked. His wings fluttered.

"Are you a fairy?" Violet whispered.

"Yes," said the fairy. "My name is Sprite of the Green Petals from the Whispering Woods. But you can call me Sprite."

"I'm Violet," she said quietly.

"Are you eight years old?" Sprite asked.

Violet nodded slowly. *How did he know that?* she wondered.

Sprite grinned. He held out a large marble. "I got this from the toad. I think it's yours."

Violet didn't move. Was she really talking to a fairy? Could it be real?

She looked at Sprite carefully. There were no wires or strings holding him in the air. And he was solid, like a real thing. Not flat like a picture.

He must be real, Violet thought.

Violet slowly took the marble from the fairy's tiny hands.

"Thank you," Violet said.

"I'm glad I could help," Sprite said with a bow. "And now I need you to help me!"

"Me? How can *I* help you?" Violet asked.

She knew about fairies. She had read about fairies who gave out wishes. But she had never heard of a fairy who asked for help. Especially from an eight-year-old girl!

Sprite flew right up to Violet's face. His wings tickled her nose.

"You *must* help me," Sprite said. "Your world is in great danger!"

3
Sprite's Story

"**H**urry up! We must go. We've got to get started. Follow me!" Sprite said. He flew away from Violet.

Violet started to follow him. Then she stopped. *Wait a minute,* she thought. *I can't believe I'm actually listening to a fairy!*

"Stop!" Violet called out.

Sprite made a quick turn in the air and zipped back to Violet.

"We can't stop!" Sprite said. "This is too important!"

Violet crossed her arms. "I'm not going anywhere with you," she said. "Not until you answer some questions."

Sprite sighed. He flew down and landed on a rock. Then he folded his wings behind him.

"I thought you said your name was Violet," Sprite said. "People named after violets are supposed to be quiet and shy. You're very loud, you know."

Violet frowned. "I got my name because of my eyes."

Sprite flew up to Violet's face. He blew a strand of red hair away from her eyes.

"I see," Sprite said. "Your eyes are purple. Not like violets at all, though. More like blueberries."

Violet brushed Sprite away. "Never mind about my name. Why is my world in danger?"

Excited, Sprite fluttered his wings. "It's just terrible! You see, yesterday some fairies escaped from my world . . ."

"Your world?" Violet asked. "You mean in the oak tree?"

Sprite shook his head impatiently.

"The oak tree is just a door to my world," Sprite said. "I live in the Otherworld. With others like me. You call us fairies. Or pixies."

"You mean like fairyland?" Violet asked.

"Yes! Yes!" Sprite said. "That's where I live. But some fairies escaped. Now they're here in your world, and I've got to bring them back!"

"What's the big deal about some fairies escaping?" Violet asked. "You don't look very dangerous to me."

"Well, these fairies *are* dangerous. And they are not all small creatures with wings, like I am," Sprite said. "There are fourteen of them. They're all different. And they're probably making a huge mess of things. So we've got to find them right now!"

4
Pix!

Violet didn't know if she believed Sprite's story. "Why do you have to catch these fairies all by yourself?" she asked.

Sprite puffed up his chest. He pulled a round medal from a bag that hung around his waist. He showed the medal to Violet. "I am a Royal Pixie Tricker. The fairy queen chose me herself. Now, do you have any more questions, or can we go?"

Violet looked closely at the medal.

"One more question," Violet said, holding up her hand. "What's all this about a queen and you being a Royal Pixie Tricker? And why do you need *my* help?"

"The queen said that I would meet a girl who is eight years old. She told me to ask you for help," Sprite said. "I'm not sure why. She said something about an old rhyme."

"Can't you remember?" Violet asked.

Sprite's wings fluttered impatiently.

"It's too long!" Sprite said. "And it doesn't matter. I found you, didn't I? So let's go!" He tugged on Violet's purple hoodie.

"Not yet," Violet said.

"Not yet? What is it now?" Sprite asked.

"I can't just *leave*," Violet said. "I'm supposed to be playing in my backyard."

Violet pointed to the big yellow house in front of them.

"My Aunt Anne is inside," Violet said. "It's Saturday. She always watches me when my parents work on the weekend."

Aunt Anne

"So tell Aunt Anne you have to go out," Sprite said.

"She'd never let me go running off with a fairy," Violet said.

"But this is *so* important!" Sprite said. "I'm sure she'll understand."

Violet shook her head. "I can't tell my aunt about you," she said. "She wouldn't believe me."

"I'll go introduce myself, then!" Sprite said.

"No!" Violet said. She grabbed him by his tiny foot. "She'd hit you with a flyswatter. Or flush you down the toilet—or worse!"

"Boo-hoo-hoo! No help for you!"

Violet jumped at the sound of a strange voice.

The voice belonged to another fairy. He was a bit taller than Sprite, but he had no wings. He had a round face. He wore colorful clothes. There were bells on his pointy shoes, cap, and collar.

Sprite frowned. "Pix!" he yelled.

"Pix is my name. Having fun is my game!" Pix said. He danced in the grass. The bells on his shoes jingled.

Violet couldn't believe her eyes. *Two fairies in one day?*

Pix opened his hand. A pile of glittering dust appeared in his palm.

"Pix will dance. Pix will sing. Pix will trap you in a fairy ring!" Pix sang.

"Pix, leave Violet alone!" Sprite yelled.

Pix did not stop. He threw the dust into the air. The dust whirled around. It formed a big circle and then surrounded Violet.

Surprised, Violet tried to walk through the shimmering ring, but she crashed into an invisible wall. "Hey! What did you do?" she asked.

Pix grinned. "You're trapped in my fairy ring forever!"

5
The Fairy Ring

"**D**on't worry, Violet!" Sprite yelled. "All you have to do is—"

"Not so fast!" Pix said. "Pix wants to play!"

Pix sprinkled some more pixie dust, and a jump rope magically appeared. The rope was turning by itself!

Pix began jumping rope.

"This is fun!" Pix said. "Now it's your turn, Sprite! Let's have some fun!"

Sprite tried to fly away. But Pix made the jump rope twirl like a lasso.

WHOOSH! Pix wrapped the rope around Sprite.

Then Pix pulled Sprite to the ground. He danced in circles around Sprite. Soon Sprite was completely tangled in the rope.

Violet slammed her hands into the fairy ring. Nothing! She couldn't get out and help Sprite.

"Now it's time for a twirl!" Pix cried.

He yanked on the rope, and it unwound. Sprite's body twirled around and around.

Sprite was free from the rope. But he looked very dizzy.

"You'll really love this next game!" Pix said. He opened his hand. A brightly colored rubber ball appeared. "It's called dodgeball!"

Pix threw the ball at Sprite.

Sprite flew out of the way just in time.

Pix frowned. "I hate it when I miss!" he said.

Another ball appeared in Pix's hand. Pix threw the ball again. He missed. So Pix threw another ball. And another. Tiny dodgeballs flew everywhere.

Sprite flew all around the yard, trying to dodge the balls. He looked exhausted.

"Violet, help!" Sprite called out.

"How can *I* help you?" Violet called back. "I'm trapped inside a fairy ring, remember?"

"Oh, right!" Sprite said. "It's easy to get out. All you have to do is—"

Sprite dodged another ball from Pix.

"Do what?" Violet yelled.

"Jump on one— No, that's not it," Sprite said. Another ball whizzed by him.

"What do I do?" Violet asked.

"You need to close your eyes— No, that's not it, either," Sprite said. He dodged another ball.

"Come on, Sprite!" Violet cried.

"Now I remember!" Sprite yelled. "First, turn your hoodie inside out. Then wear it backward."

Violet wanted to ask him how that was supposed to get her out of the ring. But she knew there wasn't time. She quickly took off her hoodie and turned it inside out. Then she put it on backward.

Poof! The fairy ring vanished. Violet was free!

"That was easy," Violet said. "And also pretty weird!"

"Great!" said Sprite. "Now, can you please help me?"

Pix threw another ball at Sprite. Violet caught it just before it hit Sprite.

"Game's over, Pix!" she said.

Violet ran to the edge of the yard. She picked up a rubber ball that was lying there.

"I know how to play dodgeball, too," she said. "Can we play with *my* ball?"

The red rubber ball was much bigger than Pix. His eyes grew wide just looking at it.

"No thanks," he replied.

Pix opened his hand again, and more glittery dust appeared. He threw the dust over his head. "Catch you later!" he cried.

Then he disappeared.

Sprite perched on Violet's left shoulder. "Thank you," he said. He sounded tired. "Things are much worse than I thought."

"Is Pix one of the fourteen fairies who escaped from your world?" Violet asked as she put her hoodie on the right way.

Sprite nodded.

"Well, now I know why you were in such a hurry," Violet said. "Of course I'll help you find them."

6
Pixie Dust

Sprite fluttered his wings. "First, we have to catch Pix," he said. "He is going to make a real mess of things."

"What will he do?" Violet asked.

"Pix loves to play," Sprite said. "He wants everyone to play with him. He taps you on the head. Then you're under his spell. You'll want to play with him *all the time*."

"You mean you won't do homework? Or clean your room?" Violet asked.

Sprite nodded. "You won't eat. You won't sleep. You'll just play and play."

"That *is* bad," Violet said.

Sprite flew back and forth nervously. "So let's find him! Take me to a place where kids like to have fun. That's probably where Pix will be."

"I will," Violet said. "But not yet."

Sprite rolled his eyes. "What is it now?"

"I can't just leave my yard and walk all over town by myself," Violet said.

Sprite flew over to a window in the house. Inside, there was a boy with curly hair playing a video game. "Maybe *he* can come along and help us," Sprite said.

"No way!" Violet said quickly. "That's my cousin Leon. He'd just spoil everything."

"Well, it doesn't matter," Sprite said. "I think I have something that will help."

Sprite opened the tiny bag that hung around his waist. He pulled out a handful of glittering dust.

Violet stepped back. "Are you going to trap me in a fairy ring with that?" she asked.

Sprite laughed. "No," he said. "Pixie dust is good for lots of things, not just fairy rings."

"Like what?" Violet asked.

"I can sprinkle some on us. Then we can go anywhere we want in seconds," Sprite said. "Just like Pix did."

"Cool!" Violet said. "We can catch Pix fast if we do it that way. We'll be back before Aunt Anne misses me."

"Right!" Sprite said. "So are you ready?"

"I think so," Violet replied. "Does this stuff really work? I'm not going to disappear forever, am I?"

"It works just fine!" Sprite promised. "Where should we go first?"

"Well, Pix likes dodgeball. Maybe we can go to a place where kids play games like that," Violet said. "We can go to the ball—"

Sprite didn't wait for Violet to finish. He quickly blew the pixie dust over both of them.

At first, the dust just made Violet sneeze. Then she felt her body tingle like a million tiny feathers were tickling her skin.

The backyard disappeared. Violet saw sparkling white lights.

Then the lights faded and the tingling stopped.

Splash! Violet felt water sloshing in her shoes.

Violet blinked. They were at the *mall*. Right in the middle of the wishing fountain!

She was standing knee-deep in water. A big statue of a fish squirted water on top of her head.

Sprite flew next to Violet's face. He was nice and dry.

"I said *ball*, not *mall*. I wanted us to go to the ball field," Violet said.

Sprite shrugged. "Sorry," he said. "I'm kind of new at this."

"What do you mean?" Violet asked. Then she heard a familiar laugh.

It was her friend Brittany Brightman.

Violet tried to duck behind the fish statue. But she was too late.

"Violet!" Brittany cried. "What are you doing in the mall fountain?"

7
No Work! Just Play!

Violet had to think fast. If Brittany found out about Sprite, he wouldn't stay a secret. Brittany was in charge of the second-grade newspaper. She'd put Sprite on the front page!

And Violet did not know what would happen if other people found out about Sprite. They might be afraid. They might put Sprite in a jar. Or in a zoo!

So Violet grabbed Sprite and shoved him into the pocket of her hoodie.

"Violet? What are you doing in the mall fountain?" Brittany asked again.

"Hi, Brittany," Violet said. "I'm just, uh . . . uh . . ."

"Going for a swim!" Sprite whispered.

"Going for a swim!" Violet repeated, without thinking.

"Ha ha," Brittany said. "Very funny, Violet."

Violet blushed. "Just kidding," she said. "I, uh, dropped something in here."

"Oh," Brittany said. She looked at her friend strangely. "You'd better get out of there. I think there are bugs in that fountain. I saw one flying near your head before."

Violet gasped. *Brittany must have seen Sprite! But she thought he was a bug.*

"Bugs, right," Violet said. "Don't worry. I'll be fine."

"I've got to go," Brittany said. "I've been waiting forever to get someone to help me in the shoe store. The workers are acting really weird today."

Brittany went back to the shoe store across from the fountain.

Violet crouched behind the fountain. She pulled Sprite from her pocket.

Sprite frowned at Violet as he smoothed out his wings. "What did you do that for?" he asked. "It was very cramped in there."

"I did it so no one would see you," Violet said. "We should try using the dust again. We have to find Pix."

"I think he's here," Sprite said. He pointed to the shoe store.

The workers weren't helping customers. They were playing catch with a shoe! Angry customers yelled at them. But the workers didn't care. They kept on playing.

"Pix must have tapped them on the head," Sprite said. "He's moving fast. Soon he will have everyone in town under his spell!"

"We should look for him," Violet said.

She stood up just as a woman's voice blared over the loudspeakers.

"This is the mall manager," the woman said with a giggle. "The mall is closed! No work today! Just play!"

"I think we're too late," Violet said. "Pix has already caused trouble! Everybody here wants to play instead of work."

"He is probably headed somewhere else," Sprite said. He reached in his bag and pulled out more pixie dust. "Where should we go?"

"How about the playground?" Violet said. "There are lots of games to play there."

Sprite blew the pixie dust on them. Violet sneezed. She closed her eyes.

The mall disappeared. Violet's skin tingled again. When Violet opened her eyes, she gasped.

8
Lost

All Violet could see was fog. Thick, gray fog.

Sprite flew in front of her. She could barely see him. She could only see his shimmering wings.

"Where are we? What happened?" Violet
asked. "Did you make another mistake?"

"I'm not sure what happened," Sprite said.

"Maybe we should try to get out of this
fog," Violet said. "Sit on my shoulder so I
don't lose you."

Violet felt Sprite land on her shoulder. She took a step forward. The thick fog swirled around them. Violet couldn't see a thing.

Violet took one step. Then another.

She stopped.

"This is no good," Violet said. "I don't even know where we are."

Sprite's tiny ears perked up. "Do you hear that?"

Violet listened. She thought she heard kids laughing and playing.

"I think we're near the playground," Sprite said.

"You might be right," Violet said. "So how did this fog get here? Did Pix make it?"

Sprite shook his head. "Pix can't do this kind of magic. But Hinky Pink could."

"Hinky who?" Violet asked.

"Hinky Pink. He's another fairy who escaped," Sprite said. "He can control the weather. He could be trying to keep us from catching Pix."

Violet shivered. The fog felt cold and clammy.

"Can't we undo the magic?" Violet asked. "I could turn my hoodie inside out again."

"That won't work," Sprite said. "This magic is too strong for that."

"Then what can we do?" Violet asked.

"There is one thing," Sprite said. "We can try saying Hinky Pink's name backward. Three times."

"Backward?" Violet asked. She tried to picture the name in her mind. "You mean we have to say 'Knip Yknih'?" Her tongue tripped over the words.

"That's it!" Sprite said. "But we have to do it together."

"Slowly!" Violet said.

Violet's and Sprite's voices rang out in the fog, "Knip Yknih. Knip Yknih. Knip Yknih!"

A strong wind came. It blew the fog away.

Violet blinked. Now the sun shone brightly in her eyes. The sky was blue. There were no clouds in the sky. It was magic!

The playground fence was right in front of them.

"We did it!" Sprite said. He pointed at the playground. "And there's Pix!"

9
Pix Power

"Quick! Let's hide!" Sprite said.

He flew behind a tree. Violet followed.

Sprite peeked at the playground. It was crowded with children.

"What's Pix doing?" Violet asked.

"It looks like he already tapped the kids in the playground," Sprite said. "They're under his spell."

Violet looked out from behind the tree. Children were playing and laughing. They swung on the swings. They slid down the slide. They went around and around on the merry-go-round.

Pix sat on one end of a seesaw. A little boy sat on the other end. Pix laughed as the seesaw flew up and down.

Violet turned to Sprite. "I don't get it," she said. "They all look like they're having fun."

"Look closer," Sprite said.

Violet looked again. Then she understood. The kids didn't look happy. They all looked tired. Their eyes looked glazed, like they were sleepwalking.

"That's not normal," Violet said.

A mom ran up to a little boy on the swing. She tried to pull him off. But the little boy cried and shouted.

The mom looked worried. Pix hopped off the seesaw. He snuck up behind her and tapped her on the head.

Then the mom laughed. She sat down on another swing.

"Let's play!" she said.

Violet frowned. "Pix is going to have *everybody* under his spell! How can we stop him?"

Sprite looked down at his shoes. "I'm not really sure," he said.

"Not sure!" Violet said. "I thought you were a Royal Pixie Tricker."

Sprite blushed. But he didn't blush pink. He turned a brighter shade of green. "I *am* a Royal Pixie Tricker," he said. "But there's so much to remember. It all gets mixed up in my head."

Violet sighed. *We have to think of a way to break Pix's spell*, she thought.

"I know!" Violet said. "What if we get everybody to turn their hoodies and jackets inside out? And wear them backward? It worked before."

Sprite looked troubled. "That *could* work. But I'm not sure."

"It's worth a try," Violet said. "You can whisper in the kids' ears. You can tell them what to do—just like you whispered to me in the fountain."

"All right," Sprite said. "I'll do it!"

"Wait a minute," Violet said.

Sprite flew back to her. He landed on a tree limb.

"I changed my mind," Violet told him. "Pix might see you if you go in there. He might do something to hurt you. Or turn you into something."

Sprite put his hands on his hips. "He can't harm me. I'm a Royal Pixie Tricker!"

"But he did trap you before, and you need to stay safe," Violet said. "You're the only one who knows how to trick all the fairies. You can hide in my pocket."

Sprite frowned. "And what will *you* do?"

"I will talk to each of the kids on the playground. If Pix spots me, I'll just pretend I'm one of the kids he put under his spell," Violet said.

"Hmm. I don't know," Sprite replied. "Pix has powerful magic. And he might remember you from before."

"You can be on the lookout for Pix," Violet said.

"All right," Sprite said finally. "But be very careful."

Sprite hopped into her pocket. Violet stepped out from behind the tree.

She opened the playground gate and snuck inside.

10

Under a Spell

Violet ran behind the slide.

She really didn't want Pix to see her.

But Pix didn't notice Violet at all. He was too busy playing! He ran to the sandbox. He jumped in. He threw sand in the air and laughed.

Violet climbed up the ladder of the slide. A little girl sat on top. She looked about five years old.

Violet tugged on the girl's shirt. "Listen to me," she said. "You're under a spell. That pixie wants you to play forever."

"I'm having fun!" the little girl said. She slid down the slide, away from Violet.

Violet slid down after her.

Maybe some of the other kids would listen.

She walked to the merry-go-round. Two boys her age were pushing it.

"You're under a spell!" Violet told them. "Turn your jackets inside out. Then wear them backward. You can break the spell!"

"Who cares?" said one of the boys.

"Yeah, we're having fun!" said the other.

They jumped on the merry-go-round.

Violet didn't know what to do.

No one wanted to listen to her. They were all under Pix's spell.

Violet stopped. She looked around her. The kids looked tired and sweaty. One little boy was leaning against a tree. He looked so worn out!

I have to do something, Violet thought. *But what?*

Then she heard the sound of bells behind her.

Bells? Did Pix find me? she wondered.

"Violet, duck!" Sprite yelled before she could turn around.

At the same time, pixie dust shot up out of her pocket. It tickled her nose!

Violet sneezed.

Violet looked down at her pocket. Sprite's head peeked out. He looked worried.

"What just happened?" Violet asked.

"Pix was about to tap you!" Sprite said. "I sprinkled pixie dust on you, so you would sneeze and duck your head."

Then Violet understood. Sprite's idea had worked! Her sneeze kept Pix from tapping her. Pix had almost put her under his spell!

"Thanks, Sprite," Violet said.

But then— "Watch out!" Sprite yelled.

Pix jumped off a swing. He started to dance. He danced closer and closer to Violet.

"Soon you'll play with me forever!" Pix said in a singsong voice.

Violet thought fast. Then she had an idea.
I'll say Pix's name backward three times,
Violet thought. *Just like with Hinky Pink.*

Violet pointed at Pix.

"Xip! Xip! Xip!" she yelled loudly.

11

The Book of Tricks

Nothing happened.

Pix laughed. "Saying my name backward won't stop *me*, Violet!" he said. He tugged at the leg of Violet's pants. "Come and play! Have fun with Pix!"

Violet shook her leg. Pix tumbled off.

Violet ran back to the playground gate. Sprite flew out of her pocket.

"The backward magic worked on Hinky Pink, but it didn't work on Pix!" Violet told Sprite.

Sprite's wings fluttered nervously.

"I don't know why it didn't work," Sprite said. "Maybe Pix's magic is even stronger than Hinky Pink's fog."

"You said you are a Royal Pixie Tricker, right?" Violet asked. "Do you know what to do?"

Sprite avoided Violet's eyes. "I *do* know what to do," he muttered. "It's on the tip of my wings . . ."

Then he smiled. "Of course! The book!"

Sprite dug into the bag around his waist. He pulled out a tiny book with a gold cover.

Violet leaned over and looked at the book. She could just make out the title.

"*The Book of Tricks*," she said. "What is it?"

"There's only one way to send a fairy back to the Otherworld," Sprite said. "With a trick."

"I get it," Violet said. "You're a Royal Pixie *Tricker.* So this book tells you how to trick the escaped fairies, right?"

Sprite nodded. "Yes. There is a different trick for each fairy."

"Why didn't you think of this sooner?" Violet asked.

Sprite blushed bright green again. "I told you. I'm sort of new at this."

Sprite opened the book. He turned the pages quickly.

"Pix . . . Pix," Sprite said. "Oh, here it is! There's a rhyme."

Sprite read the poem out loud.

Pix loves nothing more than fun.

Give him some work and his fun is done!

"Give him some work," Violet repeated. "You mean we have to make Pix do work? Like chores?"

"Yes," Sprite said.

"And then what happens?" Violet asked.

"Then a tunnel will appear and pull Pix back into the Otherworld," Sprite said. "The spell will be broken."

Violet felt a little better. It was nice to know exactly what to do.

There was only one problem.

"How are we supposed to get Pix to do work?" Violet asked. "All he wants to do is play."

12
Tricking Pix

"**I**'m sure we can find a way to get Pix to work," Sprite said. "We just need to think!"

Pix ran up to Violet and Sprite.

"There's no way to escape, Violet! Play with Pix!" he cried.

Pix jumped up to pat Violet on the head. She swatted him away. When his feet touched the ground, he pushed Violet. She magically flew through the air and across the playground. She landed on the seesaw.

"Ow!" Violet yelled.

Pix hopped on the other end of the seesaw.

"Pix loves the seesaw!" he cried. "Up and down! Up and down!"

Violet felt sick to her stomach. They were going too fast.

Sprite flew to her. "Hold on tight, Violet!" he cried.

How can we stop Pix? Violet wondered. *We have to find a way to trick him.*

"Up and down! Up and down!" Pix yelled. Suddenly, it came to her.

"Sprite!" she cried. Then she lowered her voice to a whisper. "Keep Pix busy. I know what to do."

"Got it!" Sprite said, and he flew away.

Sprite yelled at Pix. "Hey, Pix! Come over here! I've got something really fun to show you."

Pix hopped off the seesaw. He ran over to Sprite.

"What is it, Sprite?" Pix asked. "Are you still trying to catch me? Because it's no use."

"I know," Sprite said. "I just thought you'd like to see a cool trick."

Sprite took a gold yo-yo from his magic bag. He dangled the yo-yo in front of Pix. Then Sprite made the yo-yo spin up and down.

Pix's eyes lit up. "Give it to me! Pix wants to play!"

Sprite threw the yo-yo to Pix.

Pix started doing tricks with it.

Violet saw Pix playing with the yo-yo. She had to move fast.

Violet jumped off the seesaw. She looked around the playground.

She found what she was looking for. A broken branch from a tree. It was long and thick. Just perfect.

Violet ran back to the seesaw. It was empty.

She stuck the tree branch in the middle of the seesaw. She put it right in the part that makes the seesaw go up and down.

Then she yelled, "Oh no! The seesaw's broken!"

Some of the kids ran over to her. They tried to move the seesaw up and down. It was stuck.

One of the little kids began to cry.

Pix heard the noise. He threw down the yo-yo.

"What's this?" he asked. "No crying. Time to play with Pix!"

"But the seesaw's broken," Violet said. "We can't play on it."

Pix shrugged. "So what? There are other things to play on."

"But the seesaw is the best thing in the whole playground," Violet said.

Pix raised his eyebrows. "It is? Why?"

"Because you get to play with your friend," Violet replied.

"That's true. Playing with friends is the most fun," Pix said. "Pix doesn't like to play alone. You see, I don't have any friends. That is why I make everyone play with me!"

"But back in the Otherworld, you have loads of friends," Sprite reminded him.

"I'll play on the seesaw with you," Violet said. Then she sighed. "I wish I knew how to fix it."

Pix ran to the seesaw. "Maybe it just needs a little push!" he said.

Pix climbed up to the end of the seesaw. He jumped up and down on it.

The seesaw didn't move.

"Drat!" Pix said.

Pix hopped off the seesaw. He walked underneath it.

"I see the problem," Pix said. "There's a tree branch stuck in here."

Pix grabbed the tree branch. He pulled and pulled. He groaned.

"Pull harder!" Violet cried.

Little beads of sweat popped up on Pix's face. He pulled with all his might.

At last, the branch came loose.

"I did it!" Pix said. "I fixed the seesaw!"

I did it! Violet thought. *I made Pix do some work!*

Suddenly, a cold wind kicked up. The wind blew all over the playground. Violet's hair whipped around her face.

The wind formed a tunnel in the air. Right behind Pix.

The wind tunnel swirled and swirled. It pulled Pix back, back, back into the tunnel.

"Pix doesn't like this game!" Pix cried.

The sparkling wind pulled Pix farther into the tunnel.

The tunnel closed up. Then it disappeared. Pix was gone!

13
One Down

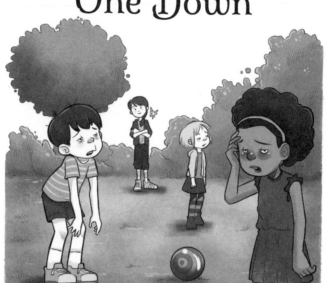

The kids on the playground looked funny. Like they had just woken up. They slowly walked off the playground.

"I'm hungry!" one little girl whined.

"I want a nap!" wailed a little boy.

The spell was broken!

"Did we really do it?" Violet asked. "Did we send Pix back to the Otherworld?"

Sprite opened *The Book of Tricks.* Above Pix's rhyme was a blank square.

Violet watched as a picture slowly formed on the page. It was a picture of Pix!

"Wow! Why did his picture just appear?" Violet asked.

Pix loves nothing more than fun.
...rb and his fun is done!

"Pix's picture disappeared from the book when he escaped," Sprite explained. "Now it's here. It means we sent Pix back."

"He looks happy in the picture," Violet said.

Sprite nodded. "He's back with his friends."

"Good!" Violet said. She watched as Sprite closed the book. "That's one down, thirteen to go."

"Right!" Sprite said. "So we should get moving!"

"Hold on," Violet said. "We can't look for more pixies right now."

"We can't?" Sprite asked. "Why not?"

"Aunt Anne will be calling for me," Violet said. "I have to eat dinner with her and Leon. After that, I need to shower and go to bed."

Sprite sighed. "You humans have so many rules."

"Those tricky pixies will just have to wait," Violet said.

"Maybe," Sprite said. "Or maybe not."

Sprite pointed to something just above Violet's head.

Violet looked up. A black cloud hung in the air. But the rest of the sky was sunny and blue.

Cold raindrops fell from the cloud. Right onto Violet's head.

Violet groaned. "Let me guess," she said. "Hinky Pink!"

Sprite tried to hide a smile. He flew outside the raindrops.

"See, Violet?" Sprite said. "The pixies won't stop causing trouble until we trick them all!"

Violet thought about the idea of tricking thirteen more pixies. She was a little scared. But mostly excited.

Sprite and I saved the world from Pix, she thought. *I was braver than I ever knew I could be.*

"Don't worry, Sprite," she said. "We'll find Hinky Pink and the other escaped fairies. We *will* trick them all!"

About the Creators

Tracey West has written several book series for children, including the *New York Times*-bestselling Dragon Masters series. She is thrilled that her first series, Pixie Tricks, is being introduced to a new generation of readers.

Xavier Bonet lives in Barcelona, in a little village near the Mediterranean Sea called Sant Boi. He loves illustrating, magic, and all retro stuff. But above all, he loves spending time with his two children—they are his real inspiration.

Pixie Tricks
Sprite's Secret

Questions and Activities

When Violet first meets Sprite, she looks at him closely to decide if he is real. What makes her think he is real? Reread page 6.

Violet knows that Pix likes to play, so she looks for him at the playground. Where else might be a good place to look?

At the playground, Violet thinks the kids are having fun when she first sees them. What makes her realize something is wrong?

Pix loves to play. Violet and Sprite can only stop Pix by making him do *work*. The words *play* and *work* are *antonyms*. This means they have the opposite meaning. *Up* and *down* are also antonyms. Make a list of all the antonyms you know.

Sprite is from the Otherworld. What do *you* think this world looks like? Draw a picture of the Otherworld. Show the pixies who live there!